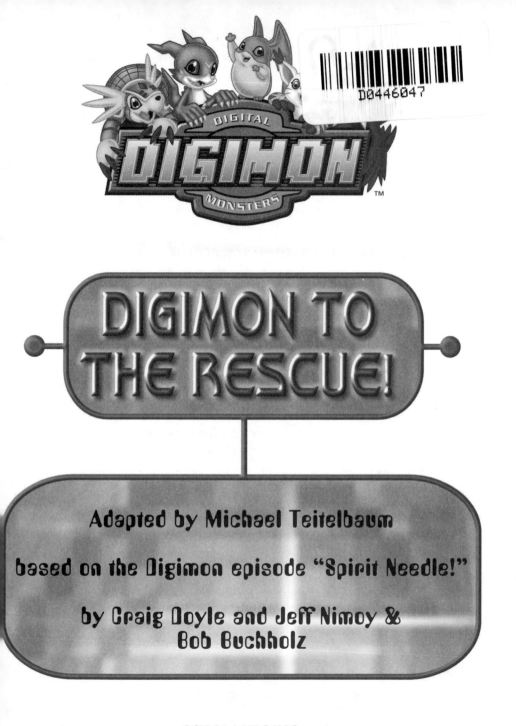

DIGITAL DIGIMON MONSTERS

DIGIMON TO THE RESCUE!

Adapted by Michael Teitelbaum

based on the Digimon episode "Spirit Needle!"

by Craig Doyle and Jeff Nimoy &
Bob Buchholz

SCHOLASTIC INC.
New York   Toronto   London   Auckland   Sydney
Mexico City   New Delhi   Hong Kong   Buenos Aires

No part of this work may be reproduced in whole or in part, or stored in a retrieval system, or transmitted in any form or by any means, electronic, mechanical, photocopying, recording, or otherwise, without written permission of the publisher. For information regarding permission, write to Scholastic Inc., Attention: Permissions Department, 555 Broadway, New York, NY 10012.

ISBN 0-439-32113-1

12 11 10 9 8 7 6 5 4   1 2 3 4 5 6/0

Printed in the U.S.A.
First Scholastic printing, September 2001

Mimi, Palmon, and a group of their tiny Digimon friends sat around a campfire and toasted marshmallows. They were having a great time.

"May I please have a marshmallow, Mimi?" asked one of the Digimon.

"Coming right up," Mimi replied.

An evil Digimon named Golemon appeared in the woods. He raced to a nearby dam.

"Oh, no," Mimi cried. "Golemon is going to break the dam. The water will flood the whole town! But I cannot stop Golemon alone. I need help!"

Mimi's cry for help was heard by her friends Yolei, T.K., Kari, Cody, and Davis. They came with their Digimon pals.

"What is wrong, Mimi?" Davis asked.

"It is Golemon," Mimi explained. "He is going to destroy the dam and flood the town!"

"Do not worry," Davis said. "Our Digimon will stop Golemon!"

The Digimon swung into action.
Pegasusmon and Nefertimon soared
into the sky.
"Golden Noose!" they shouted.

Together, the two Digimon used their Golden Noose power to create a rope made of golden energy. Then they wrapped the golden energy rope around Golemon.

"My turn!" Raidramon shouted. "Thunder Blast!"

Raidramon used his Thunder Blast power. He tossed glowing red balls of energy at Golemon.

"Rock Cracking!" called out Digmon.
He launched his Rock Cracking power.
Metal cones hurtled toward Golemon.

"Time for my Double
Stars!" Shurimon added.
Then he tossed two
spinning stars of power
right at Golemon.

The Digimon's combined powers struck Golemon. But they all bounced right off his stone body.

"Our powers did not stop Golemon at all!" Raidramon cried.

"He is too strong!" shouted Pegasusmon. "The Golden Noose is the only thing that might stop him!"

Pegasusmon held his end of the golden rope tightly.

Golemon raised his strong
arms and shook the golden rope.
Pegasusmon was tossed aside.
Golemon broke free of the
Golden Noose.

Golemon reached out
with his big, rocky fist.
Punching as hard as
he could, he blasted a
hole in the dam.
Water poured out of
the hole in the dam.
"Oh, no," Cody cried.
"There must be millions
of gallons of water!"

Mimi and her friends watched in horror as the water rushed through the forest.

"All that water is heading toward the town," Mimi said. "The whole town will be flooded!"

"We have to stop it!" shouted Raidramon.

"I will take care of this!" announced Nefertimon.

She leaped into the air shouting, "Queen's Paw!"

Using her Queen's Paw power, she sent energy beams toward the dam.

The energy beams flew through the air.
When they struck the hole in the dam, water
stopped rushing out.

Golemon roared.

"Take that, you big rock head!" Kari shouted.

No more water came out of the dam.
But the water that raced through the
forest was still enough to flood the town.
The Digimon moved quickly, speeding to
get ahead of the rushing water.

Working together, the Digimon came up with a plan to stop the water.

"Double Stars!" shouted Shurimon. His spinning stars sliced through a line of trees.

Next, Raidramon used his power to lift the trees high into the air.

Pegasusmon used his power
to bind the trees together.
They now formed a thick wall
of branches and leaves.

Using his great power, Pegasusmon placed the wall of trees right in the path of the rushing water.

"That should stop the water," he said. "It's up to you now, Digmon!"

"Rock Cracking!" shouted Digmon.
He released his Rock Cracking power.
The ground split open, forming a huge
crack right in front of the line of trees.

Digmon looked up.
The powerful flood of water
was almost on top of him.
Pegasusmon swooped
down and grabbed Digmon.
They flew to safety, just as
the water reached the trees.

The water could not get past the line of trees.

The water flowed into the large crack that Digmon had opened in the ground. Soon all the water had disappeared.

"That was awesome!" Davis shouted.

"That is what I call teamwork," Mimi said. "None of us could have done it alone. But all of the Digimon working together stopped the flood and saved the town!"